Disneynature
AFRICA
CATS

A LION'S PRIDE

Adapted by Cathy Hapka
Photography by Keith Scholey, Natasha Breed, Owen Newman,
Marguerite Smits van Oyen, and Oliver Scholey

Special thanks to Keith Scholey
Copyright © 2011 Disney Enterprises, Inc.
All rights reserved. Published by Disney Press, an imprint of Disney Book Group. No part of this book may be reproduced or transmitted in any form or by any means, electronic or mechanical, including photocopying, recording, or by any information storage and retrieval system, without written permission from the publisher. For information address Disney Press, 114 Fifth Avenue, New York, New York 10011-5690.
Printed in the United States of America
First Edition
1 3 5 7 9 10 8 6 4 2
Library of Congress Control Number on file.
ISBN 978-1-4231-4218-8
J689-1817-1-11001
For more Disney Press fun, visit www.disneybooks.com

Disney PRESS
New York

Another morning dawns on the vast African plains. A pride of lions is ready for the day.

This group lives on the savanna, a grassy plain with few trees. They are near a river where the lions often meet other animals.

There are six lionesses and one male lion called Fang in the pride. There are several cubs, too. Life is not always easy. The pride must work together to find food and water in order to survive.

The cubs are still young enough to live on their mothers' milk. But the adult lionesses must hunt if they want to eat.

Lions hunt other animals on the plains. When the dry season comes, these creatures travel to find enough food and water. The lions must stay on their own land, near the river.

Soon food becomes difficult to find, so the pride searches together. Lions often walk for two hours at a time. Mara, one of the youngest cubs in the pride, must work hard to keep up with the others.

The cub's mother, Layla, has spent many years on the plains. She watches out for danger and protects her cub.

The other cubs in the pride are older and larger than Mara. They play together, wrestling and leaping. Their games teach them skills they will use later, when hunting and fighting.

Sometimes Mara plays with the older cubs. Other times she runs around looking at everything. The whole world is new to her, and there's a lot to see!

The lionesses keep an eye on the cubs, stepping in if their games get too rough. Sometimes the rowdy cubs are so noisy that a male lion may become annoyed and let out a loud roar!

Fang and the adult lionesses rarely play with the cubs. They save their energy for more important activities, such as hunting. Lions often spend up to twenty hours a day resting.

Mara makes sure to rest, too. She stays close to the other lions. She is too small to travel alone.

The savanna is an enormous place, filled with many different creatures. Mara often sees lots of other animals, such as elephants.

Wildebeests are among the animals on the plains. They travel in huge herds that may number in the thousands. These horned creatures can live for more than twenty years.

Zebras also travel in herds. Each zebra's black-and-white stripes are unique and unlike any other's.

Gazelles are smaller than both zebras and wildebeests. They are also much faster. They can run up to fifty miles per hour. Gazelles can also jump very high, although not as high as the height of a full-grown giraffe.

Giraffes are the world's tallest mammals. They range in height from thirteen feet to nineteen feet. One giraffe eats hundreds of pounds of leaves each week. Giraffes must travel great distances in order to find enough food.

The plains are hot and dry as Mara's pride searches for their prey. When they reach a water source, everyone usually stops to drink. It might be a long time before the lions have another chance.

When the pride finds food, it is shared among all the lions. Sometimes other animals are hungry, too. Large crocodiles or hyenas may attack! Then Fang must protect the pride's meal.

One day Mara will learn to help her pride hunt. For now, the little lion cub is tired after a long day on the plains. Tomorrow there will be more new things to see.

 # LION FACTS

🐾 Only male lions have manes.

🐾 Females do most of the hunting for a pride.

🐾 Lions often hunt at night.

🐾 Lions spend sixteen to twenty hours per day resting.

🐾 Lions can go up to four or five days without water.

🐾 A lion can't roar until it is around two years old.

🐾 A lion's roar can be heard from five miles away.

🐾 When a lion walks, its heels don't touch the ground.

🐾 Lions can run at speeds of up to thirty-five miles per hour, but only for short distances.

🐾 At birth, the average weight of a lion cub is two to four pounds.

🐾 A full-grown male lion can weigh between 330 and 550 pounds.